I Wonder
as I Wander

Written by Gwenyth Swain
Illustrated by Ronald Himler

Eerdmans Books for Young Readers

Grand Rapids, Michigan • Cambridge, U.K.

For my mother, Mardi Coman Swain, who has passed on to me some of her love of music,
and for the late Gene Keller, who used to call me "Ornery" and "Meanness."

With special thanks to Ron Pen, director of the John Jacob Niles Center for American Music,
University of Kentucky, for his help and advice on the manuscript-in-progress.

— G. S.

For Deborah Shine.
— R. H.

Text © 2003 by Gwenyth Swain
Illustrations © 2003 by Ronald Himler
Published in 2003 by Eerdmans Books for Young Readers
An imprint of Wm. B. Eerdmans Publishing Company
255 Jefferson S.E., Grand Rapids, Michigan 49503
P.O. Box 163, Cambridge CB3 9PU U.K.

03 04 05 06 07 08 09 10   8 7 6 5 4 3 2 1

Library of Congress Cataloging-in-Publication Data
Swain, Gwenyth, 1961-
I wonder as I wander / written by Gwenyth Swain; illustrated by Ronald Himler
p. cm.
Summary: While dealing with the loss of her mother and life on the roads of Appalachia after her father becomes an
itinerant preacher, a young girl composes a song that expresses her feelings about Jesus.
ISBN 0-8028-5214-9 (alk. paper)
[1. Composers—Fiction. 2. Clergy—Fiction. 3. Folk Songs— Appalachian Region—Texts. 4. Appalachian Region—Fiction.] I Himler, Ronald,
ill. II Title.
PZ7.S969893 Iae 2003
[Fic]—dc21
2002151769

The illustrations were created with watercolor and pencil on paper.
The type was set in Poppl-Pontifex.
Book design by Matthew Van Zomeren.
Director of illustration Gayle Brown

Author's Note

Of all the folksongs collected and recorded by John Jacob Niles, none is as haunting and beautiful as the Appalachian tune "I Wonder As I Wander." The story behind this Christmas song is sketchy.

In 1933, in the midst of the Great Depression, Niles happened upon an open-air revival of sorts on the courthouse square in Murphy, North Carolina. Niles had collected many songs from people who lived in the surrounding hills and hollows, but he was still surprised to hear a pure young voice sing alone, with no accompaniment, these words:

> *I wonder as I wander, out under the sky,*
> *How Jesus, the Savior, did come for to die*
> *For poor orn'ry people like you and like I —*
> *I wonder as I wander out under the sky.*
>
> *If Jesus had wanted for any wee thing,*
> *A star in the sky, or a bird on the wing,*
> *Or all of God's angels in heav'n for to sing,*
> *He surely could have it, 'cause he was the King.*

The singer's name was Annie Morgan, and she earned twenty-five cents each time she repeated the short song for Niles. As usual, he scribbled the words and music in his own shorthand into a notebook until he could sing the song back to the young girl with no mistakes. At the time, Niles didn't think to ask Annie Morgan where she'd heard the tune or where she was going. And later, when he wanted to learn more, she had left without a trace.

This story—a work of fiction—continues the wondering; it tells the story of Annie Morgan and her song.

We've been wandering since Mama died. Up and down hills and hollers on muddy roads that chew your tires and spit them right out. Papa preaches in every little town, places with names like Willscott Mountain, Hot House, Murphy.

Nighttimes, we pull off by the side of the road. I get the front seat. Papa takes the hard bed of our old Ford truck. He don't seem to mind the hardness or even much mind where we go.

When we left our cabin, all of Mama's spring pretties—daffodils, tulips,
and snowdrops—were in bloom. I still can't figure how she could have died
in spring, when there's so much life just bursting from the ground and the
tree branches.

Papa said, "It's God's plan. He just took her sooner than we'd have liked."

I wanted to say God's planning sometimes ain't that good, but I held
my lip.

We tried to get on. But Papa's eyes started hurting when everywhere he looked he didn't see Mama where she'd always been before. His ears hurt when he woke up of a morning and she wasn't singing and fixing coffee and pancakes at the stove. His hands hurt when he felt the softness of the coverlet she'd made for their big bed.

"Ornery," he said to me one morning, "we're going a'wandering."

That was just like Papa. Making up his mind to do something all of a snap. He started calling me Ornery the same way. My real name is Annie Morgan, but the way Papa tells it Annie was too fine a name for the kind of baby I was—full of fire and vinegar. So all of a snap, he took to calling me Ornery. I've grown out of most of the fire and vinegar. But shucks if that old name hasn't stuck on me.

When we set out on the traveling life, Papa missed having company. He couldn't bear not to pick up any raggedy man or woman walking down the road.

"You never know, Ornery," he'd say, "which one of them might be Christ Jesus." He's talking about that story in the Bible, the one about the good Samaritan. That's a nice person who'd stop for a raggedy man.

I don't mind company myself, but if I didn't keep a few bits by, Papa would give away every penny we have to them poor folks. Far as I can tell, everybody's just about as poor as everybody else these days. Does that mean we're all Jesus?

Most days, Papa stops the truck in a little town or at a country church on a grassy hilltop. Then he sets to preaching. His big, big voice booms out over our heads and into the sky.

I listen for a while, but then my legs ache for moving and I walk out to where the grass grows tall. I walk along the edges of his talking until the sky is a big blue bowl fringed with green. I wonder as I wander which cloud is Mama's cloud in heaven.

Papa would talk about heaven and Jesus all the time, but it hurts him to see folks move on once they've had their fill. That's why Papa likes nothing better than a soup kitchen line. When you've got a hungry belly, you don't mind someone filling you up with talk about Jesus. We stop in the bigger towns just so Papa can preach to the hungry.

Papa says Jesus is King. I want to know how he can be a king and be the raggediest man you'd meet along the road. But I hold my lip.

Inside, with warm soup sliding down my throat, I get nervy and ask, "What kind of king is Jesus? Can he have anything he wants?"

"'Spect so, Ornery," Papa answers between slurps.

"Any wee thing?" I ask him right back.

"Well, I reckon. Jesus could have a tiny bird if he wanted. Even the stars in the sky at night would be his for the asking."

I want to ask, "Then how come he let himself go and die?" but I see the light of those stars shining in Papa's eyes. Mama always said she and Papa watched the stars at night in their courting days.

The way Papa tells it, when Mama was young and in her flash, she was the catch of the county. Her hair had the white-gold glow of fireflies at night, and she sang like an angel. Mama didn't just make songs sound nice, she made up her own tunes with pretty words that were as right as rain falling on a dusty road. Up until the day she died, a little gray wisp of herself, she was singing.

I can sing fair, but Mama said that isn't my gift. It's stringing together the words of a song that I like. Papa used to like my songs, before his ears got to hurting so bad.

We hadn't been in Murphy long when Papa began
preaching the news about Jesus right on the courthouse square.

Before you knew it a sheriff was telling us to push on. The sheriff allowed that he might let Papa preach a little longer if Papa piped down. That wasn't too likely, and I knew we didn't have a penny in our pockets for gas or food. So I called out, "Preacher! Ain't it time for a song?"

"I suppose it might be, Annie," Papa said. He only calls me Annie when he wants to make sure I'll be good.

"It's a song about Jesus," I told the crowd as faces turned my way.

I wonder as I wander, out under the sky,
How Jesus, the Savior, did come for to die
For poor orn'ry people like you and like I—
I wonder as I wander out under the sky.

If Jesus had wanted for any wee thing,
A star in the sky, or a bird on the wing,
Or all of God's angels in heav'n for to sing,
He surely could have it, 'cause he was the King.

My singing didn't do much for the sheriff. He cleared the crowd before Papa got a chance to pass the hat. I figured the scrawny fellow who hung by was a deputy, the way he scribbled in his notebook. But instead of saying, "Push on," he asked me to sing my song again. "I'll pay you twenty-five cents."

Twenty-five cents is good money. I sang that song over and over until he had it all down and could sing it right back to me. His singing was fair to middling, but he got most of it right.

*B*ack in our truck, Papa allowed as it might not be such a good thing for a preacher's daughter to be so full of wondering. But he said it was a fine song, all the same. "Your mama would have been proud, Ornery."

That's what I hope—that of all of God's angels, Mama can hear me sing.

I Wonder As I Wander

Unison

I won - der as I wan - der, out un - der the sky, how

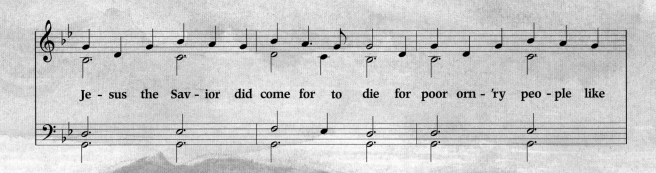

Je - sus the Sav - ior did come for to die for poor orn - 'ry peo - ple like

you and like I— I won - der as I wan - der out un - der the sky.

Appalachian carol collected and adapted by John Jacob Niles;
harmonized by Joel J. Niewenhuis

I wonder as I wander, out under the sky,

How Jesus the Savior did come for to die

For poor orn'ry people like you and like I—

I wonder as I wander out under the sky.

When Mary birthed Jesus, 'twas in a cow's stall,

With wisemen and farmers and shepherds and all.

But high from God's heaven a star's light did fall,

And the promise of ages it then did recall.

If Jesus had wanted for any wee thing,

A star in the sky, or a bird on the wing,

Or all of God's angels in heav'n for to sing,

He surely could have it, 'cause he was the King.

I wonder as I wander, out under the sky,

How Jesus the Savior did come for to die

For poor orn'ry people like you and like I—

I wonder as I wander out under the sky.